A Christmas Tree Adventure

and other Christmas Stories

Miles Kelly

First published in 2015 by Miles Kelly Publishing Ltd
Harding's Barn, Bardfield End Green, Thaxted, Essex, CM6 3PX, UK

2 4 6 8 10 9 7 5 3

Publishing Director Belinda Gallagher
Creative Director Jo Cowan
Editorial Director Rosie Neave
Senior Editor Sarah Parkin
Design Manager Joe Jones
Production Elizabeth Collins, Caroline Kelly
Reprographics Stephan Davis, Jennifer Cozens, Thom Allaway
Assets Lorraine King

ISBN 978-1-78209-828-7

Printed in China

British Library Cataloguing-in-Publication Data
A catalogue record for this book is available from the British Library

ACKNOWLEDGEMENTS
The publishers would like to thank the following artists who have contributed to this book:

Front cover: Simona Sanfilippo (Plum Pudding Illustration Agency)

Inside illustrations:
Decorative frame Rachel Cloyne (Pickled Ink)
Christmas Under the Snow Florencia Denis (Plum Pudding Illustration Agency)
A Christmas Tree Adventure Antonia Woodward (Plum Pudding Illustration Agency)
Raggedy Andy's Smile Simona Sanfilippo (Plum Pudding Illustration Agency)
The Christmas Party Charlotte Cooke (The Bright Agency)

Made with paper from a sustainable forest

www.mileskelly.net
info@mileskelly.net

Contents

Christmas Under the Snow

An extract from *Kristy's Queer Christmas*
by Olive Thorne Miller

Willie and his family live on the prairies.

*I*t was just before Christmas, and
Mr Barnes was starting for the nearest
village. "Don't forget the Christmas dinner,
Papa," said Willie.

"I hate to have you go, George," said
Mrs Barnes, anxiously. "It looks to me like
a storm. If there is a bad storm, stay in the

village till it is over. We can get along alone for a few days, can't we, Willie?"

"Oh, yes! Papa, I can take care of Mamma," said Willie.

"Well, Willie, I depend on you to take care of Mamma, and to get a Christmas dinner, if I don't get back," were Papa's last words as the faithful old horse started.

Mrs Barnes looked to where a low, heavy bank of clouds was slowly rising, and went into the snug little log cabin.

"Willie," she said, "I'm sure there's going to be a storm. You had better prepare enough wood for two or three days."

"I wish the village was not so far off," said Willie, as he came in with his last load.

Mrs Barnes glanced out of the window. Broad scattering snowflakes were silently falling. "So do I," she replied anxiously, "or that Papa did not have to come over that dreadful prairie."

Supper was soon eaten and cleared away, the fire carefully covered up, and the whole little family quietly in bed. Then the storm came down upon them in earnest.

The bleak wind howled, the white flakes came with it in millions, and hurled themselves upon that house. They piled up outside, covered the steps, and the door, and the windows, and then the roof, and at last buried it completely out of sight.

The night passed away and morning came, but no light broke through the windows. Mrs Barnes woke at the usual time, but finding it still dark and perfectly quiet outside, she turned over to sleep again. At that moment the clock struck, and the truth flashed over her.

Christmas Under the Snow

Being buried under snow is no uncommon thing on the wide prairies, and since they had wood and cornmeal in plenty, Mrs Barnes would not have been alarmed if her husband had been home. But snow deep enough to bury them must cover up all landmarks, and she knew her husband would not rest till he had found them.

"Willie," said his mother quietly, "I think – I'm afraid – we are snowed in. Light a candle and look out the window."

Willie drew back the curtain. Snow was tightly banked up against it to the top.

"Why, Mamma," he exclaimed, "How can Papa find us? And what shall we do?"

"We must do the best we can," she said.

Breakfast was taken by candlelight, dinner in the same way, and supper passed with no sound from the outside world.

It was hard to keep up the courage of the little household. Nora said that tonight was Christmas Eve, and no Christmas dinner was to be had.

A thought struck Willie that he was sure would cheer up the rest. He brought out of the attic an old boxtrap, set it on the snow, and scattered crumbs of cornbread.

In half an hour he went up again, and found to his delight that he had caught a rabbit, which had come to find food.

The rabbit was laid to rest, and the trap was set again. This time another rabbit was caught. The next catch was a couple of snowbirds. These Willie placed in a corner of the attic, using the trap for a cage, and giving them plenty

of food and water.

The snowbirds were to be Christmas presents for the girls, and the rabbits were to make a pie. As for plum pudding, of course that couldn't be thought of.

"But don't you think, Mamma," said Willie, when the girls were fast asleep, with tears on their cheeks for the dreadful Christmas they were going to have, "that you could make some sort of a cake, and wouldn't hickory nuts be good in it? I have some left up in the attic."

"Well, perhaps so," said Mamma. "If I only had some eggs – but I have heard that snow beaten into cake would make it light."

Willie cracked the nuts, then prepared the two rabbits for their Christmas dinner.

"Merry Christmas!" he called to Nora and Tot when they woke in the morning.

"See what Santa Claus has brought you!"

Before they had time to think, the girls each received their presents, a live bird, that was never to be kept in a cage, but would fly about the house till summer came, and then go away if it wished.

Pets were scarce on the prairie, and the girls were delighted. They thought no more of the dinner, but hurried to dress themselves and feed the birds, which were now quite tame from hunger.

But after a while they saw preparations for dinner, too. Mamma made a crust and lined a deep dish, then she brought something like chicken and put it in the dish with a crust, and set it to bake.

Then Mamma got out some more cornmeal, and put in some sugar and the nuts, and Willie brought her a cup of snow, which she beat into the cake, while the children laughed at the idea of making a cake out of snow. This went into the same oven and pretty soon the cake rose up light, while the pie was sending out the most delicious odours.

At the last minute, when everything was ready, Willie ran to look out of the attic skylight. In a moment there came a wild shout down the ladder.

"It's Papa!"

"Willie!" a voice called back. "Is all well?"

"All well!" shouted Willie, "and just going to have our Christmas dinner."

"Dinner?" echoed Papa. "Where is the house, then?"

"Oh, down here!" called Willie, "under the snow."

"Well, my son," said Papa, once he had climbed into the house. "You did take care of Mamma, and get a dinner out of nothing, which I am sure is delicious."

So it proved to be – even the snow pudding. When they had finished, Mr Barnes added his Christmas presents to Willie's, but nothing was quite so nice in the girls' eyes as the two live birds.

After dinner, Papa and Willie dug out passages through the snow. Then Willie made tunnels and little rooms under the snow. And while the snow lasted, Nora and Tot had fine times in the snow playhouses.

A Christmas Tree Adventure

An extract from *Captain Ted*
by Louis Pendleton

*E*verything was ready for Christmas at home – mince pies, fruit cake, a fat turkey hanging out in the cold – and no doubt the as yet mysteriously reserved presents would be plentiful and satisfactory. Only a tree was still needed, and Ted and Hubert were to get it.

So they tramped up the long hill at the back of the Ridgway farm towards the woods of evergreens and leafless maples.

The landscape as far as the eye could see was white with snow, but its depth, except in drifts, was only about two inches. Ted dragged a sled with rope to strap the tree on. Hubert trudged beside him carrying a heavy sharp hatchet.

"Aunt Mary said we must get a good one, small size, and I'm going to hunt till we do," said Ted.

About two-thirds of the way up the long white stretch of hillside, the boys paused on the brink of a pit that had been dug years before by a thick-witted settler in a hopeless quest for gold. The snows of the windy hillside had drifted into it until the bottom was deeply covered.

The boys paused to take a look into the big pit, and then continued on their way up the remaining stretch of open hillside.

They explored the woods for a quarter of a mile or more before they found just the sort of gracefully branching spruce that they wanted. In no great while this was cut down, the spreading branches were roped in, and the trunk tied on the sled, which was then dragged out into the open.

The long descent towards the distant farmhouse was gradual enough to make sledding safe. Ted declared that the easiest way to get down with their load was to slide down, and Hubert agreed.

"But we'd better look out for the pit," added Hubert.

"Oh, we'll aim so as to leave that away to one side," said Ted confidently.

And so they did. After a running start, Ted leapt on the sled, straddling the trunk of the Christmas tree, and Hubert flung

himself with a shout onto the branches.

Away they went, shouting happily, now
quite forgetting the pit in their excitement.
They only laughed when they bumped
into a snow-covered obstruction and were
swerved to the left of their intended course.
They laughed again when another bump
carried them still further to the left. A third

mishap of the same kind awoke Ted to the danger, but too late.

He had hardly begun to kick his heels into the snowy surface whirling past, in an effort to change their course, and to shout, "Look out!" in great alarm, when Hubert, whose view was obstructed by the branches of the spruce, became aware of a sudden silence and felt himself sinking through space. The younger boy scarcely realized that they had gone over the brink of the pit until he found himself floundering at the bottom in the snow, which happily was deep enough to break the force of their fall.

As soon as he found that neither Hubert nor himself had been harmed, Ted laughed over their struggles in snow up to their waists, but Hubert thought it was no laughing matter.

"We certainly were fools to try it," admitted Ted. He floundered up to a higher level of the pit's bottom, where the snow was only about two feet deep, extended a hand to Hubert, and then pulled the tree-laden sled after them.

"Now, how are we going to get out?" he asked excitedly.

"We can't get out," said Hubert, looking around at the pit's steep sides.

"But we must, Hu. Anyhow, somebody's sure to come along."

But nobody did. They shouted again and again, as time passed, and listened in vain for an answer. Meanwhile Ted tried every means of escape he could think of. He first proposed to cut steps into the side of the pit, but the hatchet could not be found. Hubert had either lost his grip on it as they were sledding down the hill, or it was now somewhere under the deep snow in the bottom of the pit.

Ted next proposed to throw the rope around a sapling that hung over the very brink some fifteen feet above their heads. He unstrapped the Christmas tree from the sled, coiled half the rope, and attempted to throw it over the sapling. Several times he succeeded in throwing the coil as high as the top of the pit, but always failed to throw it around the little tree.

"Oh, it's no use," groaned Hubert at last. "We'll never get out."

"Now, Hubert, you mustn't give up," urged Ted. "Boy Scouts don't give up. We'll get out somehow."

"But we'll have to stay here until tomorrow and we'll freeze to death. I'm nearly frozen now."

"Hubert, you quit that," rebuked Ted. "Jump up and down and swing your arms if you're cold, but don't do the baby act."

Hubert was silenced. He exercised his numb limbs, as advised, and watched Ted as he prepared to try out yet another plan.

With his pocket knife, Ted picked stones out of the side of the pit until he found one he thought might serve his purpose – an oblong, jagged bit of rock around which the rope could be securely tied. Again and again Ted threw this stone – the rope trailing after it – without succeeding in sending it around the sapling.

The Sun had set and Hubert's teeth chattered, when, almost ready to give up, it occurred to Ted to toss the stone up with both hands and all his strength, aiming half a foot to the right of the leaning sapling. This carried the stone higher than it had gone before and, at the second trial, it struck the incline above the tree, rolled and came down on the other side, carrying the rope around the trunk and bringing it within reach of Ted's hand. He drew it down and tied the two ends together.

Within five minutes Ted had clambered out of the pit. Then Hubert began his struggle to follow, but Ted stopped him, insisting that both the sled and the Christmas tree be drawn out first. Then Hubert, with the rope tied round his waist, was hauled to the upper level after much effort and some strain on the part of both the boys.

"I'll never slide down that hill again," vowed Hubert, as they neared the cheeringly lit farmhouse, dragging the sled and tree.

But Ted only said, "I'm glad we managed to get out without help."

Raggedy Andy's Smile

An extract from *Raggedy Andy Stories*
by Johnny Gruelle

*R*aggedy Andy's smile was gone. Not entirely, but enough so that it made his face seem one-sided. If one viewed Raggedy Andy from the left side, one could see his smile. However, if one looked at Raggedy Andy from the right side, one could not see his smile. So Raggedy Andy's smile was gone.

It really was not Raggedy Andy's fault.

He felt just as happy and sunny as ever. And perhaps he would not have known the difference had not the other dolls told him he had only one half of his smile left.

Nor was it Marcella's fault. How was she to know that Dickie would feed Raggedy Andy orange juice and take off most of his cheery smile?

And besides, taking off one half of Raggedy Andy's smile, the orange juice left a great brown stain upon his face.

Marcella was very sorry when she saw what Dickie had done. But Dickie's only sorrow was that Raggedy Andy was taken from him, and he could not feed Raggedy Andy more orange juice.

Raggedy Andy's Smile

Marcella kissed Raggedy Andy more than she did the rest of the dolls that night. She hung up a tiny stocking for each of the dollies, and placed a tiny china dish for each of the penny dolls beside their little spool box bed. For, as you probably have guessed, it was Christmas Eve, and Marcella was hoping Santa Claus would see the tiny stockings and place something in them for each doll.

Then, when the house was very quiet, the French doll told Raggedy Andy that most of his smile was gone.

"Indeed!" said Raggedy Andy. "I can still feel it. It must be there."

"Oh, but it really is gone!" Uncle Clem said. "It was the orange juice."

"Well, I still feel just as happy," said Raggedy Andy, "so let's have a jolly game of some sort! What shall it be?"

"Perhaps we had best try to wash your face," said practical Raggedy Ann. She always acted as a mother to the other dolls when they were alone.

"It will not do a bit of good," the French doll told Raggedy Ann. "For I remember I had orange juice spilled upon a nice white frock I had one time, and the stain would never come out."

"That is too bad," Henny, the Dutch doll, said. "We shall miss Raggedy Andy's cheery smile when he is looking straight at us."

"You will have to stand on my right side when you wish to see my smile!" said Raggedy Andy. "But I wish everyone to understand that I am smiling just the same, whether you can see it or not."

And with this, Raggedy Andy caught

hold of Uncle Clem and Henny, and made a dash for the nursery door, followed by all the other dolls.

Raggedy Andy intended jumping down the stairs, head over heels, for he knew that neither he, Uncle Clem nor Henny would break anything by jumping down stairs.

But just as they got almost to the door, they dropped to the floor in a heap, for there, standing watching the whole performance, was a man.

Raggedy Andy, Uncle Clem and Henny stopped so suddenly they fell over each other. Raggedy Andy, being in the lead and pulling the other two, slid right through the door and stopped at the feet of the man.

A cheery laugh greeted this, and a chubby hand reached down and picked up Raggedy Andy and turned him over.

Raggedy Andy looked up into a cheery little round face, with a little red nose and red cheeks, and all framed in white whiskers that looked just like snow.

Then the little round man walked into the nursery, and picked up all the dolls and looked at them. He made no noise when he walked, and this was why he had taken the dolls by surprise at the head of the stairs.

The little man with the snow-white whiskers placed all the dolls in a row, and from a little case in his pocket he took a tiny bottle and a little brush. He dipped the little brush in the tiny bottle and touched all the dolls' faces with it.

He had purposely saved Raggedy Andy's face until last. Then, as all the dolls watched, the cheery little white-whiskered man touched Raggedy Andy's face with

the magic liquid. The orange juice stain disappeared, and in its place came Raggedy Andy's rosy cheeks and cheery smile.

Turning Raggedy Andy so that he could face all the other dolls, the cheery little man showed him that all the other dolls had new rosy cheeks and newly painted faces.

Henny, the Dutch doll, was so surprised he fell over backwards and said, "Squeak!"

Then the little man put something in each of the tiny doll stockings, and something in each of the tiny china dishes for the two penny dolls.

Then, as quietly as he had entered, he left. Raggedy Andy heard him chuckling to himself as he went down the stairs.

Raggedy Andy tiptoed to the door and over to the head of the stairs. Then he motioned for the other dolls to come.

Raggedy Andy's Smile

There, from the head of the stairs, they watched the cheery little white-whiskered man take pretty things from a large sack and place them about the chimneyplace.

'He does not know that we are watching him,' the dolls all thought to themselves.

But when the little man had finished his task, he turned and laughed right up at the dolls, for he had known that they were watching him.

Then the little man swung the sack over his shoulder, and with a whistle he was gone – up the chimney.

The dolls were very quiet as they walked back into the nursery and sat down to think it all over. And as they sat there thinking, they heard the distinct *tinkle, tinkle, tinkle* of tiny sleigh bells, growing fainter and fainter as they disappeared in the distance.

The dolls all climbed into their beds, just as Marcella had left them, and they all pulled the covers up to their chins.

And Raggedy Andy lay there, his little shoe button eyes looking straight towards the ceiling, and smiling a joyful smile – not a half smile this time, but a full-size smile.

The Christmas Party

By Frances Elizabeth Barrow

*M*r and Mrs Percy had seven grandchildren – Mary, Carry, Thomas, Willy, Bella, Fanny, and finally Sarah. She was the youngest of the children, and they all loved her very much.

The children and their parents had been invited to eat Christmas dinner with their grandma. They were glad, for they liked to go to their grandma's very much.

At last Christmas Day came. The children all got to their grandma's very nearly at the same time. The first thing they did was to run up to their grandma, and wish her a Merry Christmas and kiss her. They did the same to their grandpa, then they all hugged and kissed each other, and little Sarah was almost crazy with delight.

Soon the bell rang for dinner. First they had some soup. The children did not care for soup. Then they had some roast beef and a turkey. The children all took turkey.

Then came something that was quite astonishing. It was a great plum pudding all on fire! It blazed away terribly, and Willy thought they had better send for the fire engines to put it out. But it was blown out easily, and the children each had a very small piece.

Very soon they got up and went upstairs to the parlour. In the middle of the room there was a large table covered with a cloth.

Willy said, "Grandma, that table looks as if something was on it."

And little Sarah said, "Grandma, I guess Santa Claus has been here."

"Yes," said their grandma, "Santa Claus has been here, and this time he looked like your grandpa. He will be up soon, and then we will see what is on the table."

Oh, how the children did wish to peep! They could not look at anything else. They danced and jumped round the table, and were in a great hurry for their grandpa. In a few minutes he came into the room, and went to the table and took the cloth off.

The table was covered with beautiful things, and under it was something that looked like a little red-brick house.

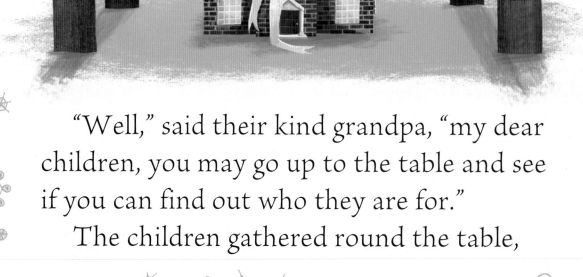

"Well," said their kind grandpa, "my dear children, you may go up to the table and see if you can find out who they are for."

The children gathered round the table,

and Willy took from the top a fine boat with all her sails set. His eyes sparkled when he saw written on a slip of paper, which lay on the deck, 'For my dear Willy'.

"It is a ship of war," said Willy, "look at the brass guns on her deck! Thank you, dear Grandpa. What is the name of my ship?"

"Her name is painted on her stern," said his grandpa. Willy looked and saw that she was called the 'Louisa'. The other children laughed, for Willy knew a very pretty little girl whose name was Louisa, and he liked her very much.

After they had all admired the boat, they went back to the table, and there were two beautiful picture books, one for Bella and one for Mary. Next to these was a large doll for Carry and another for Fanny.

The girls hugged their dolls, and then ran

to hug and kiss their grandpa. Carry said, "My dolly's name shall be Rose," and Fanny said, "My dolly's name shall be Christmas, because I got her on Christmas Day."

Thomas found for him a splendid zoo, and all the animals made noises like real animals. There were lions, tigers, hyenas, monkeys, bears, and many other wild beasts. Oh, how pleased Thomas was!

Little Sarah did nothing but jump up and down and say, "So many things! I never saw so many things!"

But who was to have the little house under the table? There was a little piece of paper sticking out of the chimney, and Sarah pulled it out and carried it to her grandpa. He took her up in his arms and read it to her. It said, "A little house for my little darling Sarah."

"It is for me," said the little girl. "My name is Sarah, and it must be for me."

Her grandpa drew the little house out and opened it. The whole front of the house opened, and there were two rooms – one was a parlour and one a bedroom. The children all cried out, "Look at the table, and the red velvet chairs, and the elegant curtains! Oh, how beautiful it is!"

Little Sarah did not say a word. She jumped up and down, her eyes shining like diamonds. She was too much pleased to speak. At last she said, "There is a young lady sitting in the chair with a red sash on. I think she wants to come out."

"You can take her out," said her grandpa.

So Sarah took the young lady out, and then took up the chairs and sofa, one by one, and smoothed the velvet, and looked at the little clock on the mantelpiece, and opened the little drawers of the bureau, then she began to jump again.

There was never such a happy party before. The children hardly wished to dance, they were so busy looking at their presents. But after a little while they had a very nice dance.

It was now quite late, and little Sarah had fallen asleep on the sofa, with the young lady out of the little house clasped tight. So they wrapped Sarah up in a great shawl, the rest put on their nice warm coats, and after a great deal of hugging and kissing, they went home happy and delighted.

So ended this joyful Christmas Day.